D0530065

For all my family   *MH*

For Dee   *CW*

Reprinted 1997

First published in 1995 by Magi Publications
22 Manchester Street, London W1M 5PG

This edition published 1997

Text © 1995 Martin Hall
Illustrations © 1995 Catherine Walters

Martin Hall and Catherine Walters have asserted their
rights to be identified as the author and illustrator of this
work under the Copyright, Designs and Patents Act, 1988.

Printed and bound in Italy by Grafiche AZ, Verona

All rights reserved

ISBN 1 85430 164 0

Charlie and Bethan

by Martin Hall

illustrated by Catherine Walters

It was spring, and lambing time high up in the dark mountains. The weather was still cold and a blizzard was raging, so the farmer was out, tending his flock.

The farmer stopped and listened. What was that? A little plaintive, bleating cry.

It was a tiny lamb, alone and hungry.

"My, you're a small one," he said. "Can't find your mother, eh? Never mind, you come home with me."

In the farm kitchen the farmer's little daughter, Emily, made the lamb a cosy nest from a cardboard box and some old jumpers. He was very weak, but was soon hungrily sucking warm milk from a bottle with a teat on it.

"Let's call him Charlie," said Emily. Then, because they could find no ewe to look after him, Charlie became the family's own special pet, and lived with them in the farmhouse.

The farmer had a sheepdog called Bethan, and as soon as
Charlie was able to skip and frisk around the farmyard, Bethan
was there to look after him. She made sure he did not stray too
far from home, and led him back there when it was time to eat.
And when Charlie was too old for the milk bottle, Bethan
showed him the best pastures to graze in.

All the time Charlie grew quickly.
He was soon too big for the kitchen,
so he slept outside in Bethan's kennel.
It was a tight squeeze, but the sheepdog
and the lamb didn't mind. For they were
friends, and kept each other warm.

They played together, when Bethan was not working.
The farmer would throw a ball and watch them both chase it.
Charlie was slower than Bethan, of course, but often she would
let him win.

"Sometimes I wonder if Charlie is turning into a dog," the
farmer's wife said, as the family watched him one day.

Charlie even had his own collar and lead. When the farmer's wife took Emily down to the village with Bethan, Charlie would go as well. The people in the shops would laugh and point, as Charlie walked proudly along the road, carrying a newspaper in his mouth.

All too soon Charlie grew too big for the kennel. It was time for him to join the other sheep.

Up on the mountainside Charlie missed his adopted family. Bethan was lonely as well without her friend, and cried by her kennel.

"Never mind, old girl," soothed the farmer. "We'll see Charlie soon enough when we have to move the flock to the next pasture."

That was when the trouble started. When the farmer and Bethan came to move the sheep to a new field, Charlie wanted to help.

"Charlie! Go back to the other sheep," laughed the farmer. But Charlie was determined to round up the sheep with Bethan, and the farmer had to push him back to the flock again.

This went on all the summer, because Charlie thought he was a sheepdog.

Summer turned to Autumn, and then it was nearly
Winter again. Charlie sniffed the air. It reminded him of a
time long ago, when he was lost and alone and cold. The sky
filled with clouds the colour of slate.

It grew colder and colder as the wind blew. The sheep
huddled together, but there was little shelter. Then it began
to snow.

Charlie baaed anxiously. Light snow began to settle on his fleece. Where was Bethan? Where was the farmer? If they didn't come soon, then snow would bury the whole flock.

At the edge of a steep slope he looked down. He could just see the farm, but the blizzard had already been there and covered everything. Charlie felt very frightened indeed, for now Bethan and the farmer would not be able to reach them.

The snow blew into the sheeps' eyes and stung them with the cold. Some of the weaker ones could barely walk through the thickening snow. Charlie knew that they must all move down into the valley, before it was too late.

Charlie ran ahead of the flock, but they stood stock-still, for they thought only a sheepdog could round them up. Luckily Charlie knew exactly what to do. He baaed loudly. He ran back and butted them, and pulled at their fleeces with his teeth. He raced backwards and forwards, until the flock began to move, all the way down the mountainside to shelter.

Many hours later the storm died down, and a low sun shone orange across the snow-covered hills. The farmer was at last able to go out and search for his flock. He paused for a moment, looking up.

"I'm really worried – I don't know if we will be able to find them," he said to Bethan. "The snow must be even deeper up there."

Bethan ran on ahead. The farmer pushed on a little way and then stopped. Was that noise just the wind? He shook his head. It must have been. As he began to struggle up the mountainside, Bethan started barking and tugging at his trousers with her teeth.

"What have you found, girl?" he asked.

Bethan led the way down again, along a thin path through some large rocks. At the end of the path the farmer stood, amazed.

All of the flock was safely gathered there, in a sheltered hollow.

"This must have been you, Charlie," he said. "You really are a sheepdog after all!"

"Woof!" Bethan agreed.

"Baa," said Charlie proudly.